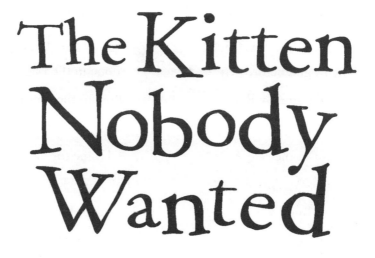

The Kitten Nobody Wanted

Pet Rescue Adventures:

Max the Missing Puppy

Ginger the Stray Kitten

Buttons the Runaway Puppy

The Frightened Kitten

Jessie the Lonely Puppy

Harry the Homeless Puppy

Lost in the Snow

Leo All Alone

The Brave Kitten

The Secret Puppy

Sky the Unwanted Kitten

Misty the Abandoned Kitten

The Scruffy Puppy

The Lost Puppy

The Missing Kitten

The Secret Kitten

The Rescued Puppy

Sammy the Shy Kitten

The Tiniest Puppy

Alone in the Night

Lost in the Storm

Teddy in Trouble

A Home for Sandy

The Homeless Kitten

The Abandoned Puppy

The Curious Kitten

The Rescued Kitten

A Kitten Named Tiger

The Puppy Who Was Left Behind

The Kidnapped Kitten

The Seaside Puppy

Also by Holly Webb:

Little Puppy Lost

The Kitten Nobody Wanted

by Holly Webb
Illustrated by Sophy Williams

tiger tales

For everyone remembering a much-missed cat

tiger tales
5 River Road, Suite 128, Wilton, CT 06897
Published in the United States 2015
Originally published in Great Britain 2011
by Little Tiger Press
Text copyright © 2011 Holly Webb
Illustrations copyright © 2011 Sophy Williams
ISBN-13: 978-1-58925-463-3
ISBN-10: 1-58925-463-5
Printed in China
STP/1000/0237/0918
10 9 8 7 6 5 4

For more insight and activities, visit us at www.tigertalesbooks.com

Chapter One

"Oh, Mia, look! I told you Mrs. Johnston had a new cat. Isn't she beautiful? So fluffy!" Mia's mom stroked the little black cat, who was sitting proudly on Mrs. Johnston's front wall.

Mia's best friend, Emily, tickled the purring cat under the chin. "She's so pretty!"

Mia's mom looked over at Mia hopefully, then sighed. She hadn't even glanced up as Mom and Emily petted the cat. She was staring firmly at her school shoes as she marched on down the road. It was as if she hadn't heard.

Mom and Emily exchanged worried looks and hurried after her. Emily lived a few houses down from Mia, and the girls usually walked to school together. Their moms and Mia's grandma took turns going with them, now that Emily's big sister, Leah, had started high school. Grandma lived in a couple of downstairs rooms in Mia's house and took care of Mia when her parents were working. She'd moved in with them a few years ago, when she'd been sick and it had been difficult for her to live on her own.

"See you tomorrow, Mia!" Emily called as she turned into her yard.

"Bye! Call me if you get stuck on that homework!" Mia was very good at math, and Emily wasn't. Emily had been complaining about their math homework all the way back from school.

Mia flung off her coat and hurried upstairs before Mom could start going on about Mrs. Johnston's gorgeous cat again. She could hear her mom asking her if she was okay, if she wanted a drink, but she ignored her.

Mia just didn't want to hear. She'd never realized before how many cats there were in her neighborhood, or on the way to school. Now that she couldn't bear to see them, there seemed to be cats everywhere.

She slumped down on her bed, and looked sadly at the navy blue fleece blanket spread over her comforter at the end. It had a pattern of little cat faces scattered on it — and there were still orange hairs clinging to it here and there. Sandy had slept on it every night, for as long as Mia could remember. She still woke up in the middle of the night expecting her old cat to be there — sometimes she even reached down to pet him, waiting for his sleepy purr as he felt her move. It was so hard to believe that he was really gone.

She looked at the photo on her windowsill. It had been taken a couple of months earlier, at the beginning of summer vacation, just a few weeks before Sandy died. He was looking thin, and they'd taken him to the vet, but that day he'd been enjoying the late summer sun in the yard, and Mia had been sure he was getting better. Looking back now, she realized that he hadn't been jumping and pouncing and chasing the butterflies like he usually did, just lying quietly in the sun. But she hadn't wanted to believe that there was anything wrong with him.

Tears stung her eyes as she stroked the glass over the photo, wishing she had the real Sandy snuggled up on her lap.

How could Mom keep pointing out other cats, and expecting her to want to stop and pet them? Dad had even suggested going to the cat rescue shelter to look for a kitten! Mia didn't want a kitten, ever. She was never going to replace her beautiful Sandy.

Mom was calling her from downstairs, asking if she wanted a snack. Brushing the tears away, Mia carefully straightened Sandy's blanket, and went down to the kitchen.

She could tell that Mom was watching her worriedly as she ate her apple. It only made her feel worse.

"Should I go and fill up the bird feeder?" Mia asked, wanting an excuse to leave the room. Mia knew Mom was only trying to help, but she really wasn't, and any minute now she was going to start talking about kittens again, or getting a rabbit, like she'd suggested yesterday.

Mia grabbed the bag of bird food from the cupboard and let herself out of the back door, taking a deep breath of relief. A blackbird skittered out of her way as she went over to refill the feeder, and she whispered to it soothingly as she unhooked the wire case.

"It's all right. I'll be gone in a minute. And I'll probably drop pieces, so you can peck them up." She poured in the seed, and then hung up the feeder and perched on the arm of the bench, shivering a little in the autumn sun. She didn't want to go back inside just yet.

All of a sudden, a damp nose butted her hand and Mia jumped, a strange, silly hope flooding into her.

But when she turned around, it wasn't her beautiful Sandy playing tricks on her. It was a pretty, plump white cat with blue eyes, and Mia recognized her: Snowball, her friend Emily's cat.

"Hi, Snowball," she whispered. "You look a bit round, kitty. Emily needs to stop giving you so many treats."

Snowball rubbed up against her affectionately. Cats always liked Mia, and Snowball knew her anyway, as Mia spent lots of time at Emily's house. Sandy had known Emily, too, although he'd always chased Snowball if she came into his yard.

This yard.

Mia swallowed and gently pushed Snowball away, then walked quickly back into the house.

Her mom was standing by the kitchen window — she'd been watching, and she sighed, very quietly, as Mia hurried back inside.

"Are you okay, sweetheart?" she asked.

"I'm going to do my homework," Mia muttered, trying not to sound tearful. She was so sick of people worrying about her. Dad had talked to her forever at breakfast that morning about Sandy. But she was perfectly all right! Why couldn't everyone just leave her alone?

Chapter Two

Mia and her grandma called to Emily on their way to school the next morning. Emily waved at them through the front window as they walked up, and then she disappeared and flung open the door.

"Guess what!" Emily shrieked.

Mia shook her head, laughing, as Emily came running down the path.

"What? You finished the math homework and it was easy?"

Emily shuddered and made a face. "No, it was awful. I don't even want to think about it. I'll have to tell you — you'll never guess. We think Snowball is going to have kittens!"

Grandma smiled delightedly, and Mia gasped. "What, really? Kittens? When will she have them?"

"We're not quite sure. Mom's going to take her to the vet today to check. We were looking at her last night, and we just realized how big she'd gotten around the middle! Mom's a little annoyed, though. Well, she's excited, but she says it's going to be a big pain, and we'll have to find homes for all the kittens." Emily frowned. "But Leah and I are going to work on Mom to let us keep one of them."

"Oh, wow…," Mia muttered. "You know, Snowball came into our yard yesterday, and I thought she was looking a little plump. But I didn't realize she was having kittens!" *I only looked at her for a minute before I pushed her away*, Mia thought, feeling guilty.

Emily chattered on happily about the kittens all the way to school, wondering how many there would be, and whether they'd be white like Snowball.

Mia joined in with a comment here and there, but thoughts were buzzing around inside her head. She still loved cats, of course she did. But it was definitely hard to be around them right now, when every cat seemed to remind her so much of Sandy. It wouldn't be so difficult if her mom and dad weren't so anxious for them to get another pet — they seemed to think Mia needed another cat to get over Sandy. And now Emily was all excited about kittens as well....

"What's the matter, Mia? You're so quiet," Emily asked, as they waved to Grandma and went in through the school gates.

Mia smiled and shook her head. "I'm fine. I'm glad I'm walking home with you and my mom today — can we stop in and see Snowball, and ask your mom what the vet said?" She was trying hard to sound excited, like she knew she should, and it must have worked, because Emily beamed at her.

"Of course you can!" Emily said, giving her a hug. "I can't wait to tell everyone about Snowball having kittens! I just hope it's true!"

Emily told Mia's mom the news as soon as they came out of school. She'd come right from work to pick them up and hadn't spoken to Grandma, so it was a total surprise.

"Oh, Mia, isn't that wonderful? Kittens!"

"Mmm." Mia tried to sound enthusiastic. She really didn't want to spoil things for Emily. "Can we see Snowball on the way home?"she asked. "Emily's mom took Snowball to the vet, so she should know for certain by now — maybe she'll even know when the kittens might be born."

Mom nodded. "Of course!"

They hurried back to Emily's house, and Emily burst through the door, racing ahead and calling for her mom. "What did the vet say? Is she definitely having kittens? When will they come?"

"Sooner than we thought!" her mom said, laughing. "Could be only a couple of weeks, the vet said. And she felt Snowball's tummy, and she thinks there are at least three kittens, possibly more."

"Three!" Emily breathed, crouching down next to Snowball, who was curled up in her furry basket. "That explains why she's so fat!"

Mia sat down next to her friend and petted Snowball gently. Her fur was beautifully soft and smooth. She wasn't asleep, but her pretty blue eyes were half-closed, as though she was tired. *She probably is*, Mia thought.

"Three kittens to find homes for," her mom sighed. She looked thoughtfully at Mia's mom. "I don't suppose...?"

Mia saw her mom smile, and glance over at her, raising her eyebrows. Emily's mom glanced at her, too, and nodded understandingly. Mia could tell exactly what Mom meant — *Maybe, but I'm not sure about Mia.*

She gave Snowball one last gentle pet. It was odd to think that there were tiny kittens squirming around inside her.

"Mom, I've got a ton of homework," she pointed out, getting to her feet. "We'd better go." They didn't really need to leave that minute, but she didn't want her mom and Emily's mom exchanging any more of those secret looks.

The subject didn't go away, though. Dad was full of questions at dinnertime, wanting to know when the kittens would arrive, and what Snowball had looked like.

"Snowball's such a sweet cat," he said, looking at Mia. "She'll have cute kittens, Mia, don't you think?"

Mia nodded. "But they won't be as beautiful as Sandy," she said, eyeing her dad firmly. "We'll never find another cat like him."

He shook his head with a sigh. "No, I suppose not. But different can be good, too, you know, Mia."

When she went up to bed that night, Mia lay there for a while, hugging Sandy's blanket and thinking. She'd never actually had a kitten of her own. Sandy had been older than she was; he was about two when she was born. Grandma had a photo of him that she kept in her living room, one that Mom and Dad had sent her when she still lived in her old house, before she came to live with them all a few years later. It was a photo of Mia as a baby, sitting up in her bouncy chair, and reaching out a fat little hand for Sandy's tail as he strolled past.

Mom had photos of Sandy as a kitten, too, in her photo album. He'd been super cute — with round green eyes that looked too big for his little whiskery face, and pink pads on his paws. They were darker by the time Mia knew him, from going outside and roughening them up. But he was still beautiful, and his eyes were like emeralds.

Mia gulped and buried her face in the blanket. It still smelled like him. She really wanted to be excited for Emily, but even the thought of kittens made her miss Sandy so much. She wasn't sure she could bear to see them for real.

Chapter Three

"I wonder if there's any news yet!" Emily said excitedly as they put on their coats at the end of school. "Mom's picking us up today. I can't wait to ask her. Snowball has been a little shy and weird all weekend, then she went off and snuggled herself up in the hall closet this morning. I'm sure that means she's 'nesting,' getting ready for her kittens to come."

It was Monday, two weeks since Emily had found out Snowball was having kittens, and she had been getting more and more impatient every day.

Mia smiled. Even though the thought of kittens made her miss Sandy, she could see how happy Emily was. They hurried out onto the playground, looking eagerly for Emily's mom. But she wasn't there. Instead, Mia's grandma was waving at them from the gate.

"Grandma! What are you doing here?" Mia called in surprise.

Grandma smiled. "Snowball is having her kittens! Your mom didn't want to leave her on her own, Emily, so she called me. My legs aren't too bad today, so I was glad to come out for a walk."

"She's having them right now?" Emily squealed in delight, whirling her schoolbag around. "Ooooh, how many are there?"

"Four so far, apparently, and your mom thought that might be it, but she wasn't sure."

"Four kittens!" Emily said blissfully, and even Mia felt her stomach squirm with excitement. "Can Mia come in and see them, Mrs. Lovett?" Emily asked Mia's grandma.

"Better not today," Grandma said thoughtfully. "They've only just been born, and Snowball will be tired and very protective of her new babies, I would think. She won't want visitors. You can tell Mia about them tomorrow."

Emily walked home so fast she was practically running, and she dashed into her yard with a wave, leaving Mia and her grandma to walk to their house.

"You're looking serious, Mia," Grandma commented. "Aren't you excited about the kittens?"

Mia was silent for a moment. The walk home and Emily's happy chattering about Snowball's babies had brought back that strange, miserable feeling again, even worse than before. It seemed so unfair that Emily should have her beautiful Snowball and four adorable little kittens, too. She wasn't jealous of Emily, exactly — just sad.

"I was," she admitted. "When you told us they were coming, I thought it was wonderful. But then Emily started talking about how sweet they'd be, and how she was looking forward to cuddling them and playing with them. And it just made mc miss Sandy so much!" She leaned her face against Grandma's arm. "I'm not even sure I want to go and see them," she whispered.

Grandma nodded thoughtfully. "I wondered if that was it. Poor Mia." She gave her a hug as they reached their driveway. "Come on. Let's go and make some hot chocolate. Maybe that will cheer you up a little."

Emily was full of news of the kittens the next day at school. Their friends Lisa and Anna rushed up to her, desperate to know what had happened. Mia did her best to join in and sound enthusiastic, but it was hard.

"There's a black one, and two tabbies, and the last one to be born was a tiny, tiny little white one, with the most enormous set of whiskers!" Emily beamed at Mia. "Do you think you can come and see them after school?"

Mia hesitated. She could — but she was worried she'd do something awful like start crying. "Um, I'm not sure," she said slowly. "Grandma's picking me up, and she said something about going shopping."

"Oh." Emily looked a bit surprised, as though she'd been expecting Mia to be more excited, and Mia felt guilty.

"Did you learn those spelling words?" she asked quickly, to try and distract Emily from the kittens.

Emily made a face. "Well, I looked at them. But the kittens were so fun to watch. They're all just nosing around each other and Snowball and squeaking. It's so funny! I probably haven't learned them correctly." She sighed. "Can you test me?"

Mia nodded, feeling relieved. She'd gotten away with it for today, but she wasn't going to be able to keep on making excuses. Sooner or later, she was going to have to go and see the kittens.

By the end of the week, Mia had run out of excuses to say to Emily, and Emily was running out of patience. On Friday at lunchtime, she told Mia that her mom said she could come over on the weekend to see the kittens if she wanted.

Mia's mind went blank. What could she possibly say, except that she didn't want to? She couldn't pretend to be busy for the entire weekend.

"So will you come?" Emily asked, staring at her and frowning slightly.

Mia opened her mouth, and then closed it again helplessly.

"You don't want to, do you?" Emily said. Her voice was flat, and Mia could see that she was really hurt. It made Mia feel terrible.

"Sorry," she whispered.

"Is it because of Sandy?" Emily said. She sounded like she was trying to be angry, but she couldn't manage it. Emily was terrible at arguing. When she and Mia had a fight, it usually only lasted two minutes before Emily cried.

Mia nodded. "It's not that I don't want you to have them. I just miss Sandy, and you having all those kittens…."

"I know you miss Sandy," Emily said, her voice getting shaky already.

"But you're supposed to be my best friend, and you should at least try to be happy for me! I really wanted to show them to you."

Mia nodded. She felt like she might cry now, too. "I know! I really am trying! I just can't make myself stop being sad about him. I can't be happy about the kittens. I can't do it!"

Emily stared back at her, tears welling up in her brown eyes, and then she gave a huge sniff and raced off to hide in the corner of the playground behind one of the benches.

Mia stared after her sadly. She knew she should go after her friend and say she was sorry, and promise that of course she'd go and see the kittens. But her feet just wouldn't move.

It was a very strange walk home. Mia and Emily didn't talk to each other, and Mia's grandma, who'd come to pick them up, could hardly get them to talk to her, either. For Mia, it was a relief when Emily ducked into her yard.

"What on earth's the matter?" Grandma asked as they took off their coats in the hallway. "Did you two have a fight?"

"Sort of…," Mia admitted.

"Well, I hope you're going to make up soon, Mia. You both looked so miserable. Can't you talk to her about it? Why don't you give her a call?"

Mia shook her head. "It wasn't really that sort of fight. We didn't yell at each other, or anything. It's mostly my fault, and Emily won't be my friend unless I can figure it out. But I can't…." She sniffed. She'd spent the entire afternoon feeling awful, and now that she was home with only Grandma to see, she felt like just letting herself cry.

Grandma hugged her. "Oh, Mia.

Why don't you tell me? Maybe talking to someone else will help."

Mia shook her head. "I don't think it will," she whispered. But she let Grandma lead her into her little living room, and sat down on the sofa with her.

Grandma gave her a tissue. "Go on, Mia. What happened?"

"She wants me to go and see her kittens."

"And you can't?"

Mia leaned against her shoulder. "It makes me too sad," she whispered. "Mom and Dad keep talking about us getting another pet, a rabbit, or even another cat. It's like everyone's forgotten Sandy."

Grandma sighed. "I don't think that's true, Mia. Your mom and dad are trying to cheer you up, that's all. We all loved Sandy, you know that. He was your special cat, though. I do understand."

"I really, really miss him...," Mia said tearfully. "Mom and Dad won't listen to me. They think I should have gotten over it by now, and I'm just being silly!"

"Oh, Mia, they really don't think that. They just want you to be happy."

"But it was August when he died, and it's only October now. I haven't stopped missing him yet." Mia sniffed. "I can't imagine not missing him! And now I can't even say anything about it to Emily, because she's so excited about her kittens. I tried to explain, but she didn't understand."

"It's such a special time for her,"

Grandma said, stroking Mia's hair. "She can't help being happy about it, can she?"

"I guess not. I just wish I could be happy with her, that's all."

"Are you sure you want to be happy?" Grandma said thoughtfully, and Mia sat up and stared at her.

"Of course I am! I don't want to be miserable!"

"But I think you're hanging onto being sad, Mia. At least if you're miserable, someone's still missing Sandy. It's as if he's still here. Do you see what I mean?"

Mia shook her head. "It isn't like that…." But her voice trailed off. Maybe it was, a little bit.

"Look." Grandma got up, and picked up a small photo album from a shelf.

"I've been making this for you, Mia, but I wasn't going to give it to you yet, in case it just made you more upset."

"Oh, Grandma! All these photos of Sandy...." Mia turned the pages, laughing as Sandy turned from a little orange fluffball into the big, handsome cat she remembered. "He was so special," she said sadly.

"Do you know what I noticed most of all about these photos?" Grandma asked, smiling at a picture of Sandy last Christmas, lying in a pile of wrapping paper, a ribbon wrapped around his paws. "He was always such a happy cat."

Mia smiled. It was true.

"Except those last couple of weeks, when he was sick. He was so tired that he wasn't really himself anymore. He'd purr if we petted him, especially for you. But most of the time, he just slept."

Mia nodded. "He didn't even want to eat."

"Exactly. And this was Sandy — he loved his food!"

Mia giggled. Mom was always getting angry with Sandy — if she left anything lying around in the kitchen while she was cooking, she only had to turn her back for a second, and a sneaky orange paw would have swiped it. He even ate mushrooms, which was very unusual for a cat.

"He wasn't happy, was he?" she muttered.

Grandma shook her head. "No. And he loved you so much, Mia. He hated it when you were miserable about something, didn't he?"

"Like that time I fell down." Mia closed her eyes, remembering. She'd fallen down the stairs and banged her arm — not actually broken it, but it had still really hurt. She'd been moping around the house with it all bandaged up, until Sandy had come and sat on her while she was lying on the sofa. He sat on her chest and stared at her, dangling his big white whiskers in her face and purring like a lawnmower. It was as though he was determined to cheer her up. And of course, it had worked!

"You're right." She turned to the last picture in the album. It was Emily and her, both holding Sandy — he was big enough for two girls to hold. They were both grinning at the camera, and Sandy looked so pleased with himself.

"Emily's your best friend, Mia. You have to make an effort for friends, even if it's hard sometimes."

Mia nodded. "I know. I'll call Emily and say I'm sorry, and I'll go and see the kittens soon. Maybe on Monday. And I'll try to stop missing Sandy so much, Grandma. I really will."

Chapter Four

Grandma must have told Mom about the talk she'd had with Mia, because on Monday morning Mom said she'd walk Mia to school, and they'd stop and pick up Emily on the way.

"Maybe you can just pop in and see the kittens," Mom suggested. "Not for long, though, because you and Emily can't be late for school. Okay?"

Mia nodded, and gave her mom a quick hug. She could see what Mom was doing. She was giving Mia a chance to see the kittens for just a couple of minutes. If it made her too sad, they could say they had to get to school.

Emily and her mom were waiting for them at the door. Mom had probably called Emily's mom, Mia decided, feeling a sudden rush of love for Mom and Grandma, worrying about her and trying to make everything okay again. The fussing had gotten on her nerves before, but they were only being nice.

"Come and see, come and see!" Emily grabbed her. "We came down this morning and they'd opened their eyes. They're so cute!" She stopped pulling Mia along and looked at her worriedly.

"You still want to see them, don't you?"

Mia nodded. "Of course. And I'm sorry I've been such a grump."

"Oh, you weren't!" Emily hugged her.

Mia was still anxious as she followed Emily into the warm kitchen. Snowball and the kittens had a little bed that Emily's mom had made out of blankets, inside a big box. It was close to the radiator to make sure the kittens stayed warm.

"Just look at them," Emily said proudly. "Aren't they the most beautiful things you've ever seen?"

Mia glanced at the bed, and Snowball yawned hugely and stared back at her. She looked as though she agreed with Emily entirely, and she expected Mia to agree, too. There was a definite look of smug pride on her pretty white face as she gazed down at her new family.

The kittens were wriggling around next to their mom. Just as Mia leaned closer, the black kitten, who seemed to be the biggest, although it was hard to tell, climbed right on top of the tiny white one, who gave an indignant squeak.

"Oh, no! Is he okay?" Mia asked anxiously, but Emily only giggled.

"I'm sure he is. They do that all the time! I wondered if it would get better when they opened their eyes, but they still just walk all over each other. And they're so greedy and pushy about getting to Snowball for their milk."

"He's the boy, isn't he? The little white one?" Emily had told Mia that they'd figured out there were three girls and one boy.

Emily nodded. "He's cute, isn't he?"

"They all are." Mia crouched down by the bed, glancing at Snowball. The white cat looked as though she was enjoying showing off her babies. The two tabby kittens were suckling, and the black one was trying to reach Snowball's side, too. But the little white kitten stayed curled up near his mom's front paws. He yawned, and then gazed up at Mia with dark blue eyes.

Mia knew that he was so small he probably couldn't see her very well, but somehow he seemed to be looking right at her, and he wrinkled his nose and meowed a tiny little meow.

Mia smiled, and reached out her fingers for the kitten to sniff. How could she have thought that anything so adorable would make her sad?

Somehow after that, Mia found that the thought of the kittens didn't upset her anymore. Maybe it was because none of them was orange, like her Sandy. They were themselves instead, and although she still missed Sandy, the kittens were so cute they mostly just made her laugh. Especially the white kitten, who seemed so loving. He always nuzzled her and licked her fingers.

One Friday afternoon, a couple of weeks after the kittens were born, Mia went to play at Emily's house. She was really looking forward to it. She'd stopped over to see the kittens quite a few times since her first visit, but only quickly. Somehow, there hadn't been a chance to spend enough time with the kittens.

Mia followed Emily into the kitchen. It had been two or three days since she'd seen the kittens, and she gasped as she got closer to their bed.

"They're so much bigger!"

Emily laughed. "I know! It's amazing, isn't it?"

Mia shook her head. "It's like someone's blown them up, like little furry balloons...." She crouched down to look more closely at the four kittens in their bed. One of the tabbies was stomping determinedly across the soft blankets on the floor, while the other three were feeding. "They look more cat-shaped, somehow. Do you know what I mean? They were just tiny fluffy balls before, but now they're mini-cats. Oh, look…."

The white kitten seemed to have heard her talking. He stopped feeding, and looked around curiously, trying to figure out where her voice was coming from. Then he stumbled toward her, uttering that tiny squeak of a meow that she'd heard before.

"Hello, sweetie," Mia whispered, and the kitten meowed back, trying to scramble up the side of the bed.

"Wow! He's never done that before!" Emily said, her eyes wide.

"Can I pick him up?" Mia asked hopefully. "Would Snowball mind?"

Snowball was still feeding one of the tabbies and the black kitten, but she had her head up, and she was watching Mia and the white kitten carefully.

"It should be okay, don't you think, Mom?" Emily asked. "We've picked them up before, and you can see he wants you to!"

Very gently, Mia reached into the bed and scooped up the white kitten, snuggling him carefully in her lap.

The kitten let out a little breath of a purr, padding at her school skirt with his paws. Then he curled up with a contented sigh. This was what he had wanted.

"He's so soft!" Mia whispered. "And I'm sure his whiskers have grown since I last saw him. Just look at them!"

The kitten stared up at her. He liked her voice. He recognized it from when she had come before, and the girl's smell. She had petted him, and he'd wanted her to cuddle him. He yawned and his waterfall of white whiskers shimmered.

"None of the others has whiskers like that!" Mia laughed. "You should call him Whiskers, Emily. You haven't named them yet, have you?"

Emily shook her head. She had a huge smile suddenly. "Well, we've only named the black kitten, because we're keeping her! She's going to be my birthday present!" She picked up the black kitten, who seemed to have fallen asleep while she was feeding. "I'm calling her Satin." She snuggled the kitten under her chin lovingly.

"You're so lucky!" Mia smiled, but her stomach turned over. Of course. The kittens would have to go to new owners. She sighed, and the white kitten made a little grumbling noise as his comfy lap shifted. She'd only known Whiskers — she couldn't help calling him that, even though she knew it wouldn't be his real name — for a couple of weeks, but already she knew she would miss him.

Chapter Five

Whiskers wriggled himself further into the cozy fold of the blanket. He was still very tiny, but he was starting to understand more about the world, and today the world felt cold. He didn't like it. Usually he would have snuggled up next to his mother, but she had disappeared. Now that he and his sisters were a little bigger, almost four weeks old, she did that every so often.

Something soft landed in the bed next to him, and Whiskers twitched and woke out of his half-doze. It was a big, round, bright pink thing. He had no idea what it was. Neither did his two tabby sisters, who prowled toward it together, hissing fiercely. They were very good at being fierce. Whiskers and Satin watched worriedly as one of the tabby kittens dabbed a paw at the pink thing. It bounced a little. She tapped it again, and it wobbled in an interesting sort of way, so she jabbed at it with her claws out.

The balloon burst with an enormous bang, and the tabby kittens jumped back in surprise, eyeing the shriveled bit of pink that was left. Whiskers cowered in the corner of the bed, meowing with fright and wishing his mother would come. He had no idea what had happened! How had the round pink thing disappeared, and why had there been that terrible noise?

Snowball shot back into the room, convinced that someone was hurting her babies, and leaped into the bed, checking them all frantically. Whiskers pressed up against her, shivering.

"I'm sorry, kittens." Emily crouched down by the bed. "I didn't mean to scare you. It was only a balloon — I'm blowing them up for my birthday party, and that pink one must have rolled off the table."

Whiskers meowed again, eyeing the other strange round pink things he could see on the kitchen table. Did that mean there were going to be more horrible noises? When Emily tried to give him a comforting pet he let her, but he was trembling, and showing his tiny little teeth.

"Oh, no...," Emily said sadly. "It really scared you, didn't it? Well, I've got some good news. Mia's coming later, and she's staying overnight. That'll be nice, won't it? You love Mia, don't you?" She sighed to herself, almost angrily. "And Mia loves you, too. She just doesn't know it yet."

Mia had been visiting the kittens almost every day, and she always went right to Whiskers. "I wish she'd just hurry up and figure out that she should take you home," Emily told Whiskers sadly. "Mom's already talking about looking for new homes for you in a few weeks. I've given Mia lots of hints, but she doesn't get them at all, and I don't want to come out and say it in case it makes her miserable about Sandy again."

She tickled Whiskers behind the ears. "You want to be Mia's kitten, don't you, Whiskers? You never play as nicely with anyone else. And you're always sad when she goes home. You meowed after her yesterday, and you looked really lonely, even though you were cuddled up next to Snowball." She sighed. "Anyway, you'll all have to be super-cute tonight for my sleepover," she told the kittens, half-seriously. "Mia's coming, and Lisa and Anna. At least, they are if it doesn't snow before then. It's so cold now! You'd better groom your babies, Snowball. Put their party fur on!"

"Oh, did you do all the balloons, Emily? Good. I'll hang them up in the hall, and you go and get changed. Leah's just putting the birthday banner on the front door." Emily's mom hurried into the kitchen and gave her a quick hug. "Are you excited about your party?"

Emily nodded, laughing. "Of course I am. But it's so chilly! I'm not sure about sleeping on the living room floor now!"

Her mom nodded. "I know. I hope

it doesn't get too much colder before Christmas. It's still only November."

Leah came in, rubbing her fingers. "I'm frozen," she moaned, but then her eyes widened. "Hey, look at Satin!"

The black kitten was teetering on the edge of the kittens' box, and as they watched, she half-jumped, half-fell onto the kitchen floor, where she stood up and shook herself, trying to look as though she meant to do exactly that.

"Oh my goodness...," Mom muttered. "We're in for it now. They'll be everywhere. We need to remember to keep the kitchen door closed."

The two tabby kittens were now standing on their back legs, peering over the top of the box and staring at their sister with huge, round eyes, as though they couldn't believe what she'd managed to do. Satin had set off to investigate the kitchen and was sniffing thoughtfully around the table legs.

"Should I let her explore for a bit?" Emily asked, and Mom nodded.

"I think she'll wear herself out soon. Go and get changed — your friends will be here any minute. Just make sure you shut the kitchen door!"

Mia looked at the kittens a little anxiously. Lisa and Anna had just arrived, and the kitchen had suddenly gotten very noisy. She hoped Snowball and the kittens wouldn't mind.

But Satin and the two tabby kittens were loving the attention. They put on a beautiful performance of stalking a piece of yarn, and then climbed all over Lisa and Anna. Satin then snuggled up on Lisa's knee, while the tabbies fought each other for the yarn. Only Whiskers was still in the kitten bed, hiding behind Snowball.

"The little white kitten's so cute!" Anna said, reaching into the bed to pick him up. Whiskers shied away from her, but she didn't seem to notice — she grabbed him, and took him out of his safe bed, dangling him in front of her.

"Don't scare him...," Mia said worriedly. She was itching to snatch Whiskers away from Anna. It wasn't that Anna meant to frighten him; she just didn't know how to hold him correctly. But Whiskers wasn't hers. She couldn't boss Anna around. And if Mia grabbed him, he'd only be even more scared. Emily was out of the room, helping her mom put everyone's coats away, or Mia knew she'd have said something.

Anna sat down on the floor, placing Whiskers on her lap and petting him. But he was upset now, and he hissed and dug in his claws as he scrambled to get away from the loud, scary girl.

Anna squeaked. "Ow! He scratched me!" She jerked her leg, and Whiskers slipped off her lap, landing on the floor with a worried meow.

"Sshh, sshh. Come here, Whiskers." Mia stretched out a hand to him gently, and he gladly crept over to her, burrowing into her skirt as she put him on her lap.

"He didn't mean to scratch you," she told Anna. "He's just a bit more shy than the other kittens."

Anna nodded. "He's sweet, but I like the tabby ones more. They've got such cute tricks! Oh, look! That one has yarn all wrapped around her paws!"

Mia petted Whiskers and sighed. He had cute tricks, too, like the way his huge whiskers wobbled when he yawned, and the way he always put his front paws in the food bowl, now that the kittens were starting to eat solid food. Satin and the tabbies were so much bouncier, so everyone always noticed them first.

"You need to be more friendly," she whispered to Whiskers. "You won't find an owner if you keep hiding in your bed. People will be coming to see if they want to take you home a few weeks from now. You've got to show everyone how wonderful you are."

She smiled, a little sadly. She wanted Whiskers to have a loving home of his own, but if he stayed at Emily's, it meant she'd be able to keep on seeing him. Emily's mom kept saying they were only keeping Satin, but if they couldn't find a nice owner for Whiskers, she might change her mind....

Whiskers didn't know what Mia was saying, but he liked listening to her, and she made him feel safe. He purred, very quietly, and nuzzled her hand.

"Do you want to watch the movie in our sleeping bags?" Emily asked as she took a bowl of popcorn out of the microwave. "Oh, this smells great!"

"Definitely sleeping bags," Anna agreed.

"Can we bring the kittens?" Lisa asked hopefully.

Emily's mom looked thoughtful. "I suppose, for a little while. But they'll probably want to be back with Snowball soon. And after the movie, girls, you need to go to sleep! It's getting late."

The girls all nodded angelically, but Emily winked at Mia behind her mom's back. "I've got a secret chocolate supply," she whispered. "Are you bringing Whiskers?"

Mia nodded. "If you think he won't mind. He prefers being in his bed, doesn't he?"

Emily shook her head. "Not if it's you cuddling him."

Mia's cheeks turned pink. "Do you think he likes me that much?"

Emily rolled her eyes. "Of course he does! Come on!"

Mia went into the living room, and snuggled up in her sleeping bag — even with the heat on high, it was still chilly. Emily's mom had said they'd better all sleep in a huddle to keep warm, and she'd found a bunch of extra blankets. Whiskers sat on Mia's tummy, purring quietly to himself. He was happy. He hadn't been sure about the loud girls, and people grabbing him, but now he had Mia, and she didn't seem to be going anywhere, like she usually was. He could even put up with the noisy girls if Mia was there, too.

Mia hardly paid attention to the movie at all. She was watching Whiskers, snuggled up on her sleeping bag, and petting him gently. His fur was so soft — and he was such a little cat, so different from Sandy.

As the movie went on, the other kittens padded back to the kitchen, looking for Snowball and their bed. But Whiskers curled up on top of Mia and fell fast asleep — and he was still there the next morning.

Chapter Six

"Oh, Mia!" Dad laughed. "How did you get him to do that?" He'd just arrived to pick Mia up from the sleepover. Lisa and Anna had left already; they had to hurry off to dance class.

Mia shook her head very carefully.

"I didn't, Dad. He just climbed up there. I think he's eyeing my toast."

From his place on her shoulder,

Whiskers purred loudly, and Mia giggled as his long whiskers tickled her cheek. "I wish I didn't have to go home and say good-bye to you!"

Her dad exchanged a thoughtful glance with Emily's mom. "When will the kittens be ready to go to new homes?"

"Well, I was looking it up, and it seems that about 10 or 12 weeks old would be best. Ours are four weeks now, so they'll be 10 weeks old about halfway through December. So I thought around then. It's a little close to Christmas; that's the only problem. Everyone's so busy, and I don't want to be encouraging people to give kittens as presents."

"Why not?" Mia asked. She thought a

kitten would be a wonderful Christmas present. Emily was getting Satin for her birthday, after all.

"Well, people sometimes get a kitten for their children at Christmas, and don't really think about them growing up into big cats who need care. Then sometimes they're abandoned," Emily's mom added sadly. "Luckily, most kittens are born in the spring or summer. Snowball was a bit late!"

Mia reached up and tickled Whiskers under the chin. She could feel his purrs buzzing against her neck.

I could take you home, she thought to herself, just for a second. But then she remembered. She didn't want another cat — not after Sandy. Very gently, she reached up and lifted Whiskers off her shoulder, and took him over to the bed. "I'm sorry, sweetheart. I have to go."

Whiskers stared after her in surprise. Had Mia not liked him sitting on her shoulder? Why was she going? He wailed — a loud, sad kitten wail that made Mia flinch as she dashed into the hallway to grab her stuff.

She said good-bye to Emily quickly. She felt bad rushing off, but she just couldn't stay any longer. She was almost silent on the walk home, even though Dad kept trying to ask about the party.

"Mia, have you thought…?" Dad started, as they carried her things into the house. "Emily's mom talking about homes for the kittens made me wonder. You seem to get along so well with Whiskers."

He trailed off when Mia looked up at him with her eyes full of tears.

"I can't," she whispered. "I thought I could, but what about Sandy? I'm not going to forget him! I never, ever want another cat again!"

"You don't have to forget him, Mia…," Dad tried to say, but Mia raced off upstairs to her room and slammed the door behind her.

Over the next few weeks, Emily kept Mia updated as they started to look for new homes for the kittens. Her mom had put an ad in the newspaper, and the local shops that had bulletin boards. A couple of people had called about coming to see them already.

"Someone named Maria is coming over on Saturday to see them all," she told Mia as they ate their lunches. "I'm sort of half-excited, half-sad. I really want them all to have nice homes." Emily shook her head. "And at least we're keeping Satin."

Mia nodded. She wanted them to have good homes, too. Especially Whiskers. He needed a home with somebody who could love him properly, without always remembering another cat. Sandy was her forever cat. She couldn't replace him, not even with Whiskers.

Emily's mom showed Maria into the kitchen, where Emily and Leah were playing with the kittens.

"Oh, aren't they sweet! How many are there?" Maria asked, laughing as one of the tabbies sniffed her boots.

"Four, but we're keeping Satin — the black kitten. There are two female tabbies, and the little white boy. Did you want just one kitten?" Emily's mom asked. "We're thinking that the tabby girls might want to stay together — they're such a team."

"I was only planning on getting one," Maria said. "I can't see a white kitten...."

"He was here a minute ago!" Leah looked around the kitchen. "Now that they can climb out of their bed they're all over the place."

"He's a little shy," Emily's mom explained. "But he's very sweet once he gets used to you. Look, there he is!" She smiled, and pointed to the bed, where a little white head was poking out from under the fleece blanket. "I'll get him out." She picked him up and tried to pass him to Maria, but Whiskers squeaked in fright and hissed, his paws sticking out rigidly, and his tail fluffed out to twice its usual size.

"Oh, dear. Don't make him if he doesn't want to," Maria said worriedly. "Poor thing. He really is nervous. There are a lot of cats where I live, and I'm not sure this little one would cope very well if he's so shy. I'm sorry — I'm sure you'll find homes for them all."

Emily's mom followed her to the door, and Emily and Leah looked down at Whiskers, who was now huddled in Leah's arms.

"Oh, Whiskers," Emily muttered.

"No one's going to want you if you do that every time. It's so silly! He wants to be Mia's kitten, I know he does."

Leah nodded. "I know. But we can't make her have him. Maybe she'll come around to the idea."

Emily sighed. "I wish she'd hurry up about it."

A couple of weeks later, Mia and her grandma stopped in at Emily's house on the way home from school, and found that only Whiskers and Satin were left.

"I'm not surprised Whiskers didn't like them. The two little boys were so noisy," Emily's mom was saying to

Grandma. "They thought Whiskers was adorable, and they were all set to choose him, but it was just like with Maria. They tried to cuddle him, and he actually shot out of the kitchen door, and went and hid in the closet under the stairs! So they decided they'd take the tabbies instead." She laughed. "And they're going to call them Molly and Polly. I don't think they'll ever be able to remember which is which!"

"So it's only Whiskers now?" Mia asked, as Emily's mom made Grandma some coffee. Mia sat petting the little ball of white fur curled up in her lap.

Emily nodded. "At least he still has Satin to play with. But Mom's decided that we're keeping only one. We have to find Whiskers a home, and no one wants an unfriendly kitten."

"He isn't!" Mia said indignantly. "He's a sweetheart. He's just shy." *But maybe that's a good thing*, she admitted to herself. *I really don't want him to go....*

Whiskers yawned, and wriggled himself comfortable again. Mia and Emily had been rolling balls of newspaper for Satin and him to chase, and he was exhausted. The kitchen was covered in shredded paper, though. He rolled over onto his back, all four paws in the air, showing off his fat, pinkish tummy. He was liking solid food more and more now, and after he'd had a meal, he was practically circular.

"But he's so different with you…," Emily sighed. "He doesn't mind playing with me and Leah, and he'll let us pet him. But I don't think he's ever gone to sleep on me. And definitely not upside down! That means he really trusts you, you know."

Mia nodded. She didn't dare say anything, but she looked up at Grandma. She was smiling, and nodding as if she agreed with Emily. Maybe she was being silly. Was it like Grandma had said when the kittens were born — that she was still holding onto missing Sandy? Was she making herself sad on purpose? Maybe it was finally time to let Sandy go….

Chapter Seven

"I'll come and get you at about six then, Mia," Grandma said one day after school. Grandma gave her a kiss, and Mia waved good-bye. Whiskers was already weaving himself happily around her ankles, purring. His purr had definitely gotten louder as he got bigger, Mia decided. He was 12 weeks old now, definitely old enough for a new home.

But no one seemed to want a shy, nervous little white cat. Mia didn't mind. She was looking forward to spending lots of time with Whiskers over Christmas vacation. It had even started to snow that morning, although the flakes hadn't really stuck to the ground. She was sure that Whiskers would look beautiful if they took him out to play in the snow. He would be invisible, except for his round blue eyes!

Whiskers patted at her leg with his paw, asking to be picked up. Mia came to see him almost every day now, but he still missed her when she wasn't there. One day maybe she would take him with her?

"Hello, Mister Whiskers." Mia picked him up and cuddled him.

"What should we do, hmm?"

"Homework!" Emily said, grinning and waving the sheet Mrs. Jones, their teacher, had given them for the project they had to do over Christmas vacation. It was the last week of the quarter, and neither of the girls really felt like working, but Mrs. Jones was the scariest teacher at their school. The project had to be planned, even if it was only a little more than a week until Christmas Day. "We have to figure out this project, remember? Come on. Bring Whiskers with you." She scooped up Satin, leaving Snowball alone in the hallway, looking quite relieved. Whiskers and Satin were so much bigger now, and so bouncy that they wore Snowball out.

"I can smell fish sticks," Mia said a while later. "So can Whiskers and Satin. Look at them!" The kittens were prowling up and down by Emily's bedroom door, their tails twitching eagerly.

"I think our plan sounds pretty good," Emily said, looking down at what they'd written. *'Animals in the Time of Queen Victoria.'* I'll bet no one else will have thought of that. It's a great idea, Mia."

Mia laughed. "I'll come up with the ideas, you do the writing. You almost finished the entire plan while I was cuddling Whiskers. Do you think our snack is ready? The smell of those fish sticks is making me hungry."

"Must be. Let's go and see." Emily opened the door, and the kittens shot out onto the landing and eyed the stairs uncertainly. They wanted to be down there with the delicious fishy smell — but they weren't really sure about stairs yet....

Whiskers looked at Mia pleadingly, and she laughed and picked him up. She carried him down to the kitchen, while Emily followed with Satin.

Emily's mom smiled as they came in. "Look at those kittens! I've never seen them look so hungry. We'd better find the fish-flavored kitten food."

"I think they'd rather have the fish sticks," Emily said, going to the cupboard for the can and spooning out the kitten food. "Ugh. This one smells the worst!"

But Satin and Whiskers raced to their bowls and gulped down the food eagerly.

Emily's mom had just passed Leah, Emily, and Mia their drinks when the phone rang. She went to answer it, fighting with her oven mitts. "Hello? Oh, yes…. That's right. There's actually only one kitten left now."

Mia smiled, pausing with her fork halfway to her mouth. A paw was patting her knee. Whiskers must have wolfed down his kitten food already, and now he was on the hunt for something even better. She scooped him up onto her lap, and fed him a tiny bit of fish stick. Emily's mom wasn't looking; she was concentrating on the phone call.

"Oh, you've been looking for a white kitten? That's wonderful. He's a little bit shy, though, that's the only thing. He's very friendly once he knows you, but he may not want to be picked up."

The person on the other end of the phone didn't seem to mind this. Emily's mom was nodding and smiling.

Whiskers stared up at Mia, hoping for some more fish stick. His whiskers shook with excitement as he reached up a little white paw to pat Mia's hand.

But she didn't give him any. She put down her fork, very slowly and quietly, and stared at him. The kitten's whiskers drooped. Mia's face had changed; she didn't look like the girl who'd been

93

sneaking him scraps a moment before. She was pale and miserable. Whiskers meowed, his ears flattening against his head. What was wrong?

"Tomorrow evening? Yes, that would be great. See you then." Emily's mom put down the phone, smiling. "Someone wants to come and see Whiskers! Her name's Madeline, and she says she's adopted a nervous cat before, so she doesn't mind if he's shy. And she's always wanted to have a white kitten. It's perfect!"

Emily nodded, but she was looking worriedly at Mia.

Mia gulped. Whiskers was going to have a perfect home — and it wasn't with her. She'd let this happen. If only she'd been brave enough to say that she wanted him to be her kitten — that she still loved Sandy, but she'd said good-bye to him.

She stood up jerkily, cuddling Whiskers against her tummy, and passed him to Emily. "I'm sorry, I'm not feeling very well. I have to go home," she said, hurrying to the front door.

"Mia, wait! I'll call your grandma," Emily's mom said worriedly.

"It's okay, I'll be fine," Mia called back, tears already stinging her eyes as she wrestled with the front door lock. At last it gave, and she dashed down the sidewalk.

Meowing frantically, Whiskers made a flying leap off Emily's knee and chased after Mia. Where was she going? She hadn't even tickled his ears and scratched under his chin, like she usually did when she left.

He shot out of the front door, onto the path, and looked around. He'd never been out at the front of the house, only on carefully-guarded trips into the back yard. The yard was frozen over with a layer of frost, and snowflakes were flurrying down from the darkening sky. If Mia had been with him, Whiskers would have chased the strange fluffy things, but now he hardly noticed them. He had no idea where Mia had gone. He sat down on the path and wailed miserably for her.

But Mia couldn't hear him. She was almost home now, and she could hardly see through her tears, let alone hear a heartbroken kitten halfway up the road. She pressed the front doorbell over and over until Grandma came, looking worried.

"Oh, it's you, Mia! But I was coming to get you…. Mia, what's wrong?"

"Whiskers," Mia sobbed. "I was too late for Whiskers. I should have said

I loved him, and I didn't. How could I be so silly? You were right all along, Grandma, and now I've lost him!"

Grandma hugged her. "Oh, Mia. I'm so sorry. Has someone taken him?"

Mia nodded. "A lady's coming to see him tomorrow, and she's going to love him, I know she will."

"Tomorrow?" Grandma guided her inside and shut the door. "But Mia, why don't you go back to Emily and her mom and explain? Tell them you want him."

"But I can't!" Mia wailed. "I kept saying no, because of Sandy. They'll think I'm just going to change my mind again. And I told Dad that I never, ever wanted another cat. Dad and Mom would never let me have Whiskers now." She sat down on the bottom of the stairs with her chin in her hands. "Madeline — the lady who called — said she knows all about nervous cats, and she really wants him. Whiskers deserves to have an owner like that." She sniffed. "I should have been braver before."

Grandma sat down next to her. "I do see what you mean, Mia, but I think you're being too hard on yourself — and that poor little cat." She stared thoughtfully at the front door, and a small smile curved up at the corners of her mouth.

Mia didn't see it — she had her fingers pressed against her eyes now to stop herself from crying. She could see white speckles against her eyelids, and they reminded her of kitten fur.

"Are you sure?" Emily wrinkled her nose anxiously and glanced up, checking that Mrs. Jones hadn't seen them talking. "Won't it just make you feel worse?"

Mia shook her head. "No. I really want to say good-bye to him. I have to. I probably will feel horrible, but it would be awful to never see him again."

"I guess you're right." Emily sighed. "Madeline sounded really nice, from what Mom said."

"I know," Mia whispered. Then she shook her head, trying not to think about saying good-bye to Whiskers. "We're supposed to be writing about Victorian animals. Did you bring that book from the library?"

They got back to work — Mrs. Jones had said their project idea sounded excellent. But every time she stopped writing, Mia felt sad again, remembering Whiskers's soft white fur and those amazing whiskers! He was so different from Sandy, but he was special, too. The way he always wanted to climb all over her, and his clever trick of perching on her shoulder....

He'll be too big to do that soon, though, she thought. She'd never see what he looked like as a grown-up cat! Mia swallowed miserably.

She wasn't sure if the day raced by, or if it crawled. All their classes seemed to last forever, but soon it was time to go home. It seemed like all of a sudden, she was putting on her coat and grabbing her stuff, and following Emily to meet Leah outside the gates. And the walk home seemed to vanish in seconds. Mia felt almost sick as they went into Emily's house.

She expected Whiskers to bounce up to her purring as he usually did, but the house was very quiet. Snowball and Satin were curled up together in Snowball's old basket.

Mia swallowed. "Where's Whiskers?" she asked Emily's mom.

She looked around, hoping that he was hiding, and he was going to jump out and surprise her. But really, she knew that he wasn't. "He's gone, isn't he? That lady's already come by and taken him?"

Emily's mom was starting to say something, but Mia couldn't bear to listen. She was too late — even to say good-bye!

Emily rushed over and tried to give her a hug, but Mia gently pushed her away and ran home.

Grandma answered the door, looking excited, but Mia hardly saw her. She didn't even stop to listen to what Grandma was trying to say. She simply raced up the stairs to the safety of her bedroom, flinging herself onto her bed and hugging Sandy's old blanket.

Now she had lost both of them.

Chapter Eight

Whiskers sniffed around the strange room worriedly. He didn't understand what was going on. He had been carried here in a box, and he hadn't liked it, his claws catching and scratching on the cardboard as he slid around, meowing and hissing. Then he'd been let out in this strange new place. He was sure he'd never been here before, but it smelled familiar somehow, and there was a bowl of his favorite food, and some water. The old lady had watched him, but she hadn't tried to pick him up. She'd just sat, very quietly, and every so often she whispered to him. He knew her. She came to visit with Mia sometimes — so why was she here, when Mia wasn't?

It was all very odd. He'd hoped that Mia might come and see him, after she disappeared so quickly the day before. But what if she didn't know where he was? He needed to get back home so Mia could find him.

The old lady had gone away now. She had hurried off when the doorbell rang. She'd closed the door behind her, Whiskers noticed, as he sniffed at it. Or almost, anyway. The latch hadn't quite caught. Whiskers nosed it, and it swung open a little more. The curious kitten poked his whiskers around the door, and then his nose, and then the rest of him — and set off to search for Mia....

Whiskers pattered down the hallway, his nose twitching. He felt confused. Maybe Mia had come to find him after all. He was sure he could smell her. Or was he imagining it? He looked from side to side, wondering where to go. Food smells were coming from behind him, but from the noise it sounded like there were people upstairs. Stairs....

He trotted over and looked up the flight of stairs. They were very steep.

Luckily, they had carpet, or he would never have been able to get his claws in to struggle up. Whiskers scrambled up onto the first step, feeling proud of himself. He licked his paw and brushed it over his ears to settle his fur before he tackled the next step. And the next....

It took him a few minutes to heave and claw his way up to the top, and he rolled onto the last step, panting exhaustedly. His claws ached. But he was up! And he could hear voices coming from behind a door at the top of the stairs. His ears flattened. They were not good voices. Someone was upset. The second voice was the old lady who had been with him downstairs. She was doing that gentle, soothing talking again.

The door was open a crack, and he peered cautiously around it. The old lady was sitting on the bed, with a girl lying face-down beside her, patting her hair while she cried. Whiskers sniffed again. He'd never heard Mia sound like that before, but he was sure it was Mia. Would she be glad to see him? What was the matter with her? He hesitated by the door, uncertain what to do.

Then the old lady looked up and saw him. She looked surprised for a moment, but then she smiled and held out her hand to him, rubbing her fingers together, her face hopeful.

She wanted him to come closer.

"Mia, sweetheart, listen. I've got something to tell you. I'd have told you right away if it hadn't taken me so long to get up those stairs."

"I'm sorry, Grandma. I know you're not supposed to use the stairs. Oh, I should have told Emily's mom a long time ago that I wanted Whiskers to be ours...," a muffled voice sobbed.

That was his name. It was Mia — it had to be. She smelled right, and she'd said his name, even if her voice sounded all strange.

Whiskers bounded across the bedroom and looked up angrily at the bed. How was he supposed to get up there? The old lady stretched out her hand and scooped him up, smiling. "Mia...."

He had been right! Whiskers stumbled along the soft comforter until he was next to Mia's tangle of blond hair, standing on a blue fleece blanket. He nudged her with his nose, but she didn't notice, so he did it again, harder this time.

Mia raised her head. Her eyes were blurry and sore from crying, so for a moment she didn't understand.

Then Whiskers purred at her proudly. He had found her!

"Whiskers!" Mia gasped. "What are you doing here? Why aren't you at your new home? Did you run away? Emily's going to be so worried about you." She struggled to sit up, and gazed at the little white kitten sitting contentedly in the middle of her bed.

"That's what I was trying to tell
you," Grandma said gently. "When
you came home so upset last night,
I had a talk with your mom and
dad, and we all agreed. Your dad
had been convinced that you should
have Whiskers anyway. He wanted to
bring him home a long time ago, but

your mom was worried it would upset you again. So Dad and I went over to Emily's house and talked to her mom after you'd left for school this morning. We arranged for Whiskers to be your kitten. Well, and a little bit mine, for some company while you're at school. I know you shouldn't give animals as presents, but think of him as an early Christmas gift." Grandma smiled at her, a little anxiously. "Your mom was so upset that she had to be at work this afternoon. She wanted to see your face when you found out."

"But what about the lady who called? Madeline?" Mia asked. Her mind was spinning, trying to take all this in.

"Emily's mom called her to explain. She was very sympathetic, apparently.

She lost a cat recently, too; she said she knew how hard it could be."

"So Whiskers is really ours?" Mia looked down at the kitten, who was sniffing the cat blanket interestedly, his whiskers looking remarkably white against the navy blue fleece. She reached out and tickled him under the chin, with just one finger. She didn't dare do more. She felt like there was a dream kitten in her bedroom and if she touched him, he might disappear, like a bubble.

But he didn't. He purred loudly and gazed up at her with big blue eyes. He looked very, very pleased with himself.

"Yes, you are a clever little cat, finding your way up here," Grandma said, smiling. "I thought I'd closed him in my bedroom, Mia. I didn't want him wandering all over the house, feeling lost. But he obviously found a way out. He wanted to come and find you."

Mia nodded. "He's sitting on Sandy's blanket," she whispered suddenly, a strange sharp feeling clutching at her chest.

Grandma nodded. "Yes."

Mia took a deep breath. Whiskers nudged her knee with his nose and stood up, turning around a couple of times before settling himself into the perfect position, nose touching tail tip, like a little white fur cushion.

Mia let her breath out again, shakily. There were white hairs on the blanket now, mixed with the orange ones.

Whiskers opened one eye and yawned, showing a raspberry-pink tongue. Then he snuggled down further into the blanket and went to sleep.

Just like he belonged.

Mia yawned and rolled over, and felt Whiskers sigh in his sleep beside her. She'd had to move the fleece blanket now, to the side of her bed. Whiskers liked to sleep jammed between her and the wall, even though Mia sometimes worried that she would accidentally squash him.

She buried her head in her pillow and sighed happily. It didn't feel like time to get up yet. Then her eyes snapped open. It was Christmas Day!

"Whiskers! Look, my Christmas stocking." She sat up, and eyed the bulging red-and-white striped stocking happily. She could see a bag of her favorite candy sticking out of it. "And cat crunchies! Your favorite fish ones!"

Whiskers purred with pleasure. He didn't know why Mia wanted to wake up early, but he would do anything for fish crunchies. He patted happily at the ribbons as Mia unwrapped her stocking presents.

"It's almost seven o'clock," Mia said at last. "I wonder if Mom and Dad would mind being woken up yet? Or Grandma?"

She climbed out of bed and put on her robe, then padded out to the top of the stairs, with Whiskers following her.

She peeked through her mom and dad's bedroom door, but they were both still fast asleep. Dad had said last night that his best Christmas present would be to sleep in, so she scooped Whiskers up before he could go and leap onto the bed. He'd only been with them a week, but already he had a thing about Dad's feet. He liked to pounce on them, and Mia thought that probably wouldn't be Dad's ideal way to wake up.

She crept down the stairs. Grandma always woke up early; she said it was to do with being older than 70 — she didn't need as much sleep anymore.

"I can hear you, Mia! Merry Christmas!" Grandma called, as Mia hesitated outside her door.

Mia slipped into Grandma's room.

"You're up already!" she said in surprise. Grandma was sitting in her armchair, with a magazine and a cup of tea.

"Yes, and I'm glad you're here. I've got a special present for you." Grandma reached over to her little table and picked up a flat, rectangular package, wrapped in shiny Christmas paper with a big bow. Grandma liked wrapping presents.

"'For Mia, with lots of love this Christmas — and for being brave,'" Mia read from the gift tag. "I don't understand."

"Open it, Mia. You'll see." Grandma nodded eagerly.

Mia put Whiskers down on the

floor, then started to undo the bow and peel off the paper.

"Oh, Grandma! It's beautiful!" It was a box, with a painting of a cat on the lid.

"But you haven't seen inside it yet. Open it up."

It wasn't actually a box, Mia realized, as she opened it. It was a hinged photo frame, made to hold two photos, one beside the other.

As though it was made for two very special cats.

Mia smiled, her eyes blurring a little with tears, but happy ones. On the left was Sandy, staring out at her, with his ears pricked up. *Grandma must have taken it just as he saw a butterfly to chase*, Mia thought. Sandy loved to hunt butterflies....

And on the right was a picture of her little Whiskers sitting on Grandma's windowsill. The winter sun was shining on his beautiful whiskers so that they sparkled.

"Thanks, Grandma. It's the most wonderful present." Mia hugged her, and laughed as there was a sudden rustling sound. Whiskers had jumped onto the discarded wrapping paper and was pouncing backward and forward, chasing an imaginary something. Maybe when he was bigger, Whiskers would chase butterflies, too....

Out Now:

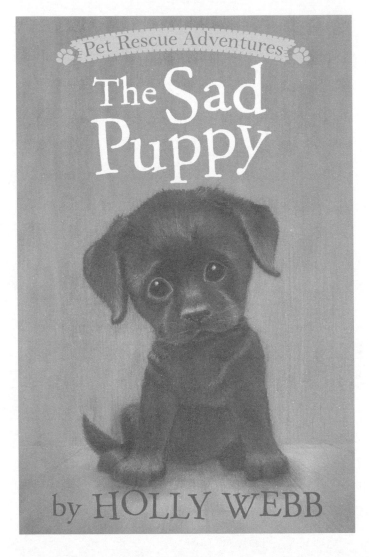

Pet Rescue Adventures

The Sad Puppy

by HOLLY WEBB

Pet Rescue Adventures

The
Abandoned
Puppy

by HOLLY WEBB

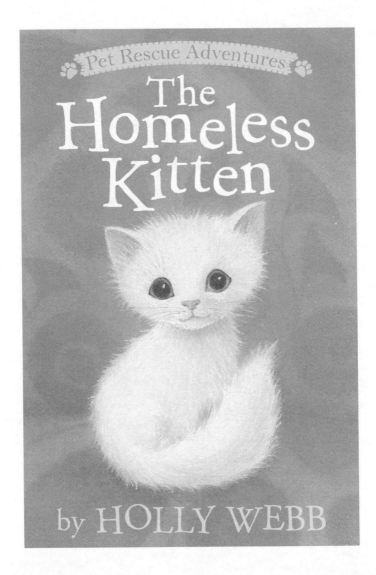

Pet Rescue Adventures

The Homeless Kitten

by HOLLY WEBB

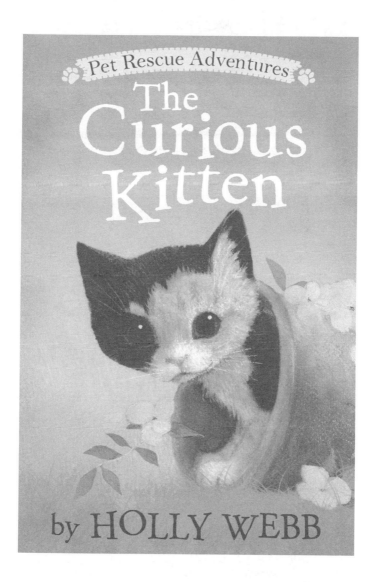

The
Curious
Kitten

by HOLLY WEBB

HOLLY WEBB

Holly Webb started out as a children's book editor, and wrote her first series for the publisher she worked for. She has been writing ever since, with more than 100 books to her name. Holly lives in England with her husband, three young sons, and several cats who are always nosing around when she is trying to type on her laptop.

For more information
about Holly Webb visit:

www.holly-webb.com
www.tigertalesbooks.com